This book belo

Cicada's SONG

Cicada's SONG

Written and Illustrated by

Ariane O'Pry Trammell

PELICAN PUBLISHING
New Orleans 2021

First edition, 2016
First Pelican edition, 2021

ISBN: 978-1-4556-2612-0

Printed in Korea
Published by Pelican Publishing
New Orleans, LA
www.pelicanpub.com

DEDICATION

This book is dedicated to my youngest son,

Gavin Dale Trammell.

Deep in the bayou,
on a warm summer night,

The owl said, "Hooo hooo!"
and the fireflies shined bright.

Boudin and T-Boy were tucked into bed.
Mama said, "Sweet dreams!"
and kissed dem both on the head.

Then, t'ru the twilight,
they heard such a noise!
"Rrreeeeeeeeeeee!"

"What you think dat could be?"
asked dem scared little boys.

Mama laughed, "Das jus' Cicada singin' a song!
He'll keep singin' dat until love come along."

For seventeen years, he hid deep in the ground,
growin' up strong and big,

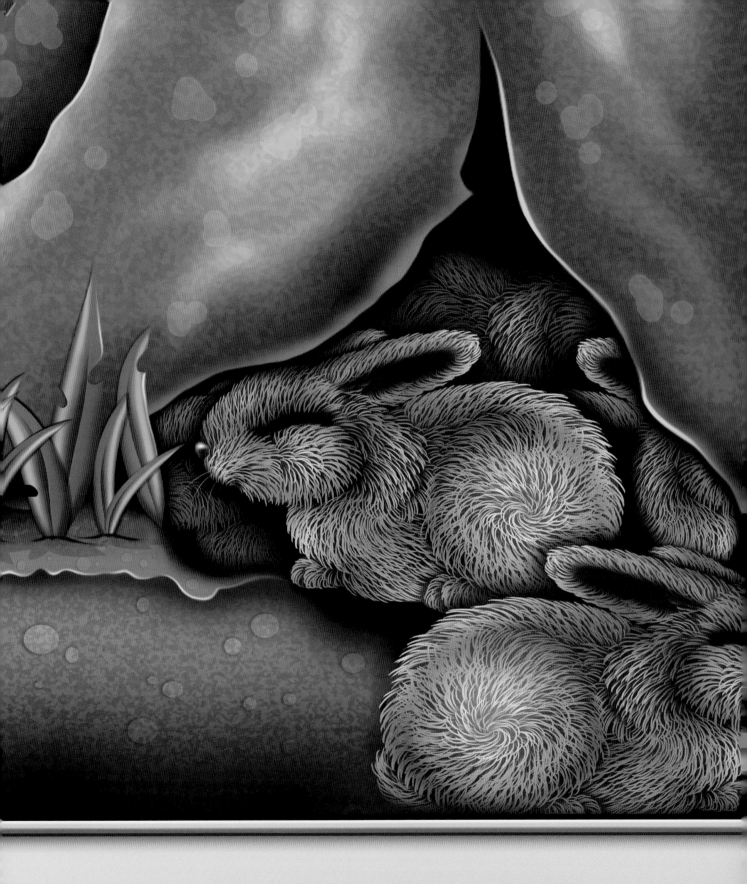

Until finally it was time to come out,
and up t'ru the dirt he dig.

He climbed way up the tallest tree
and come out of his shell.
He waited so long to spread dem new wings
and sing his song well.

"Rrreeeee!" he rang proud from upon
the highest limb.
But no other creatures wanna hear
dat noise from him!

"You quiet down!" yelled a beaver from her dam.

"Dat's WAY too loud!" yipped a fox inside his den.

Cicada kept singin' and
he sang with ALL his heart.

"Don't you know what time it is?"
squawked an egret t'ru the dark.

"RRREEEEE rrreeeeee RRREEEEEEEEEE!"
Cicada did sing.
And everybody in the swamp was
sho 'nuff listening!

"Rummmm Rum!"
a big bullfrog drummed.
"Don't you worry 'bout dem!
Your true love, she gonna come!"

"Don't be discouraged," crickets chirped,
"you charming bug!"

"RRREEEEEE rrreeeee!" Cicada sang
and waited for his love.

And to his surprise, dat angel, she come . . .

Flippin' her wing wit' a song of her own.

She landed on his branch,
and she whispered,

"Mi amour, dat's the best singin'
I done ever heard before!"

So, when you hear dat noise at night,
you don't haf'ta be scared.

After seventeen years down in the ground,
love is in the air!

About the Author/Illustrator

Ariane O'Pry Trammell is an artist and children['s] book author/illustrator from the small tow[n] of Ponchatoula, Louisiana. Having illustrat[ed] numerous publications for other authors, who[m] she guided through the process of self-publishi[ng,] she was encouraged to write a children's book [of] her own. Her first book, *Where the Grass Is Alwa[ys] Greener,* was released in 2013.

As the mother of two young sons, Kellan a[nd] Gavin, Ariane is constantly inspired to creat[e.] Often featured in her illustrations, her childr[en] are even depicted as the characters Boud[in] and T-Boy in her very successful Cajun serie[s.] She launched the first book of that series, "*R[un,] Boudin, Run!*", in 2016. *Cicada's Song* soon follow[ed] in 2017. *Couillon, the Crawfish* made its debut [in] 2018.

Ariane finds herself immensely blessed to have a career that is both her passion and a God-given gift. She is a member of the historic French Market in New Orleans, where she regularly sells her books, and she often visits schools and libraries to share her stories. She hopes to inspire, encourage, and instill a love of reading and art in every child.

Find the author online:
www.ArianesArt.com

Facebook.com/ArianeTrammellBooks

To schedule an event with Ariane,
contact her directly:
artbyariane@hotmail.com